Annie Trumbull Slosson, Alice Barber Stephens

Fishin' Jimmy

Annie Trumbull Slosson, Alice Barber Stephens

Fishin' Jimmy

ISBN/EAN: 9783337413149

Printed in Europe, USA, Canada, Australia, Japan

Cover: Foto ©Andreas Hilbeck / pixelio.de

More available books at **www.hansebooks.com**

FISHIN' JIMMY ✿ BY ANNIE TRUMBULL SLOSSON ✿ ✿ ✿ WITH ILLUSTRATIONS BY ALICE BARBER STEPHENS ✿ ✿ ✿ ✿ ✿

NEW YORK ✿ CHARLES
SCRIBNER'S SONS ✿ ✿
M DCCC XCVIII ✿ ✿ ✿

List of Photogravures

_**_* In addition to these, there are five head
and tail pieces by Alice Barber Stephens

FISHIN' JIMMY

I

IT was on the margin of Pond Brook, just back of Uncle Eben's, that I first saw Fishin' Jimmy. It was early June, and we were again at Franconia, that peaceful little village among the northern hills.

The boys, as usual, were tempting the trout with false fly or real worm, and I was roaming along the bank, seeking spring flowers, and hunting early butterflies and moths. Suddenly

Fishin' Jimmy

there was a little plash in the water at the spot where Ralph was fishing, the slender tip of his rod bent, I heard a voice cry out, " Strike him, sonny, strike him !" and an old man came quickly but noiselessly through the bushes, just as Ralph's line flew up into space, with, alas! no shining, spotted trout upon the hook. The new-comer was a spare, wiry man of middle height, with a slight stoop in his shoulders, a thin brown face, and scanty gray hair. He carried a fishing-rod, and had some small trout strung on a forked stick in one hand. A simple, homely figure, yet he stands out in memory just as I saw him then, no more to be forgotten than the granite hills, the rushing streams, the

2

Fishin' Jimmy

cascades of that north country I love
so well.

We fell into talk at once, Ralph and
Waldo rushing eagerly into questions
about the fish, the bait, the best spots
in the stream, advancing their own
small theories, and asking advice from
their new friend. For friend he seemed
even in that first hour, as he began
simply, but so wisely, to teach my
boys the art he loved. They are older
now, and are no mean anglers, I be-
lieve; but they look back gratefully to
those brookside lessons, and acknowl-
edge gladly their obligations to Fishin'
Jimmy. But it is not of these practi-
cal teachings I would now speak;
rather of the lessons of simple faith,
of unwearied patience, of self-denial

3

and cheerful endurance, which the old
man himself seemed to have learned,
strangely enough, from the very sport
so often called cruel and murderous.
Incomprehensible as it may seem, to
his simple intellect the fisherman's art
was a whole system of morality, a
guide for every-day life, an education,
a gospel. It was all any poor mortal
man, woman, or child, needed in this
world to make him or her happy, use-
ful, good.

At first we scarcely realized this, and
wondered greatly at certain things he
said, and the tone in which he said
them. I remember at that first meet-
ing I asked him, rather carelessly, "Do
you like fishing?" He did not reply
at first; then he looked at me with

Fishin' Jimmy

those odd, limpid, green-gray eyes of
his which always seemed to reflect the
clear waters of mountain streams, and
said very quietly: "You would n't ask
me if I liked my mother — or my
wife." And he always spoke of his
pursuit as one speaks of something
very dear, very sacred. Part of his
story I learned from others, but most
of it from himself, bit by bit, as we
wandered together day by day in that
lovely hill-country. As I tell it over
again I seem to hear the rush of mountain streams, the "sound of a going in
the tops of the trees," the sweet, pen-
sive strain of white-throat sparrow, and
the plash of leaping trout; to see the
crystal-clear waters pouring over granite
rock, the wonderful purple light upon

Fishin' Jimmy

the mountains, the flash and glint of darting fish, the tender green of early summer in the north country.

Fishin' Jimmy's real name was James Whitcher. He was born in the Franconia Valley of northern New Hampshire, and his whole life had been passed there. He had always fished; he could not remember when or how he learned the art. From the days when, a tiny, bare-legged urchin in ragged frock, he had dropped his piece of string with its bent pin at the end into the narrow, shallow brooklet behind his father's house, through early boyhood's season of roaming along Gale River, wading Black Brook, rowing a leaky boat on Streeter or Mink Pond, through youth, through manhood, on and on into old age, his life had apparently been one long day's fishing, — an angler's holiday. Had it been only that? He had not cared for books, or school, and all efforts to tie him down to study were unavailing. But he knew well the books of running brooks. No dry botanical text-book or manual could have taught him all he now knew of plants and flowers and trees.

He did not call the yellow spatter-dock Nuphar advena, but he knew its large leaves of rich green, where the black bass or pickerel sheltered themselves from the summer sun, and its yellow balls on stout stems, around which his line so often twined and twisted, or in which the hook caught,

7

not to be jerked out till the long, green, juicy stalk itself, topped with globe of greenish gold, came up from its wet bed. He knew the sedges along the bank with their nodding tassels and stiff lance-like leaves, the feathery grasses, the velvet moss upon the wet stones, the sea-green lichen on boulder or tree-trunk. There, in that corner of Echo Lake, grew the thickest patch of pipewort, with its small, round, grayish-white, mushroom-shaped tops on long, slender stems. If he had styled it Eriocaulon septangulare, would it have shown a closer knowledge of its habits than did his careful avoidance of its vicinity, his keeping line and flies at a safe distance, as he muttered to him-

Fishin' Jimmy

self, "Them pesky butt'ns agin!"
He knew by sight the bur-reed of
mountain ponds, with its round, prickly
balls strung like big beads on the stiff,
erect stalks; the little water-lobelia,
with tiny purple blossoms, springing
from the waters of lake and pond.
He knew, too, all the strange, beauti-
ful under-water growth: bladderwort
in long, feathery garlands, pellucid
water-weed, quillwort in stiff little
bunches with sharp-pointed leaves of
olive-green, — all so seldom seen save
by the angler whose hooks draw up
from time to time the wet, lovely
tangle. I remember the amusement
with which a certain well-known botanist, who had journeyed to the mountains in search of a little plant, found

9

Fishin' Jimmy

many years ago near Echo Lake, but
not since seen, heard me propose to
consult Fishin' Jimmy on the subject.
But I was wiser than he knew. Jimmy
looked at the specimen brought as an
aid to identification. It was dry and
flattened, and as unlike a living, growing plant as are generally the specimens
from an herbarium. But it showed the
awl-shaped leaves, and thread-like stalk
with its tiny round seed-vessels, like
those of our common shepherd's-purse,
and Jimmy knew it at once. " There's
a dreffle lot o' that peppergrass out in
deep water there, jest where I ketched
the big pick'ril," he said quietly. " I
seen it nigh a foot high, an' it 's juicier
and livin'er than them dead sticks in
your book." At our request he ac-

Fishin' Jimmy

companied the unbelieving botanist and myself to the spot; and there, looking down through the sunlit water, we saw great patches of that rare and long-lost plant of the Cruciferæ known to science as Subularia aquatica. For forty years it had hidden itself away, growing and blossoming and casting abroad its tiny seeds in its watery home, un- seen, or at least unnoticed, by living soul, save by the keen, soft, limpid eyes of Fishin' J i m m y. A n d he knew the trees and shrubs so well:

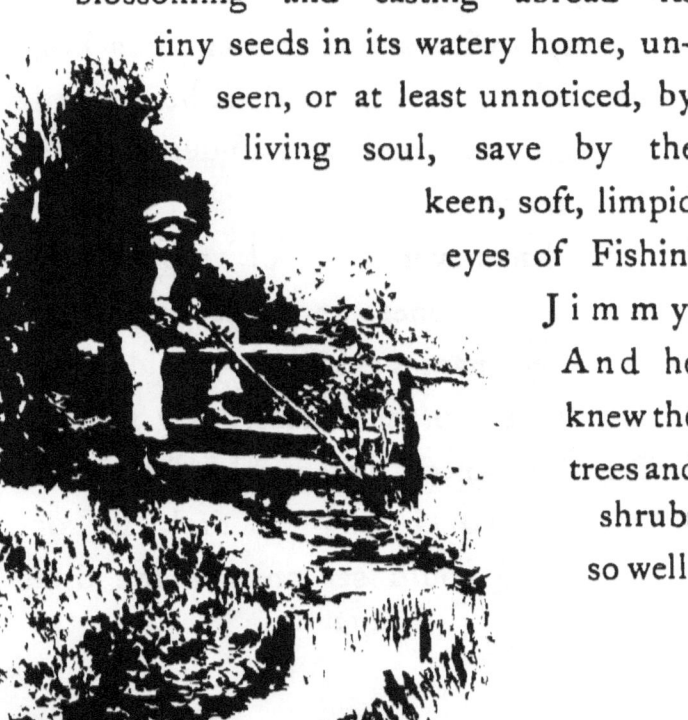

Fishin' Jimmy

the alder and birch from which as a boy he cut his simple, pliant pole; the shad-blow and iron-wood (he called them, respectively, sugarplum and hardhack) which he used for the more ambitious rods of maturer years; the mooseberry, wayfaring-tree, hobble-bush, or triptoe, — it has all these names, — with stout, trailing branches, over which he stumbled as he hurried through the woods and underbrush in the darkening twilight.

He had never heard of entomology. Guénée, Hübner, and Fabricius were unknown names; but he could have told these worthies many new things. Did they know just at what hour the trout ceased leaping at dark fly or moth, and could see only in the dim

Fishin' Jimmy

light the ghostly white miller? Did they know the comparative merits, as a tempting bait, of grasshopper, cricket, spider, or wasp; and could they, with bits of wool, tinsel, and feather, copy the real dipterous, hymenopterous, or orthopterous insect?

And the birds : he knew them as do few ornithologists, by sight, by sound, by little ways and tricks of their own, known only to themselves and him.   The white-throat sparrow with its sweet, far-reaching chant; the hermit-thrush with its chime of bells in the calm summer twilight; the vesper-sparrow that ran before him as he crossed the meadow, or sang for hours, as he fished the stream, its

13

Fishin' Jimmy

unvarying, but scarcely monotonous little strain ; the cedar-bird, with its smooth brown coat of Quaker simplicity, and speech as brief and simple as Quaker yea or nay ; the winter-wren sending out his strange, lovely, liquid warble from the high, rocky side of Cannon Mountain ; the bluebird of the early spring, so welcome to the winter-weary dwellers in that land of ice and snow, as he

 " From the bluer deeps
 Lets fall a quick, prophetic strain,"

of summer, of streams freed and flowing again, of waking, darting, eager fish, the veery, the phœbe, the jay, the vireo, — all these were friends, familiar,

Fishin' Jimmy

tried, and true to Fishin' Jimmy. The cluck and coo of the cuckoo, the bubbling song of bobolink in buff and black, the watery trill of the stream-loving swamp-sparrow, the whispered whistle of the stealthy, darkness-haunting whippoorwill, the gurgle and gargle of the cow-bunting, — he knew each and all, better than did Audubon, Nuttall, or Wilson. But he never dreamed that even the tiniest of his little favorites bore, in the scientific world, far away from that quiet mountain nest, such names as Troglodytes hyemalis or Melospiza palustris. He could tell you, too, of strange, shy creatures rarely seen except by the early-rising, late-fishing angler, in quiet,

Fishin' Jimmy

lonesome places : the otter, muskrat,
and mink of ponds and lakes, — rival
fishers, who bore off prey sometimes
from under his very eyes, — field-mice
in meadow and pasture, blind, bur-
rowing moles, prickly hedgehogs,
brown hares, and social, curious
squirrels.

Sometimes he saw deer, in the early
morning or in the dusk of the evening,
as they came to drink at the lake shore,
and looked at him with big, soft eyes
not unlike his own. Sometimes a shaggy
bear trotted across his path and hid
himself in the forest, or a sharp-eared
fox ran barking through the bushes.
He loved to tell of these things to us
who cared to listen, and I still seem to

Fishin' Jimmy

hear his voice saying in hushed tones, after a story of woodland sight or sound : " Nobody don't see 'em but fishermen. Nobody don't hear 'em but fishermen."

II

BUT it was of another kind of knowledge he oftenest spoke, and of which I shall try to tell you, in his own words as nearly as possible.

First let me say that if there should seem to be the faintest tinge of irreverence in aught I write, I tell my story badly. There was no irreverence in Fishin' Jimmy. He possessed a deep and profound veneration for all things spiritual and heavenly ; but it was the veneration of a little child, mingled as is that child's with perfect confidence and utter frankness. And he used the dialect of the country in which he lived.

"As I was tellin' ye," he said, "I allers loved fishin' an' knowed 't was the best thing in the hull airth. I knowed it larnt ye more about creeters an' yarbs an' stuns an' water than books could tell ye. I knowed it made folks patienter an' commonsenser an' weather-wiser an' cuter gen'ally; gin 'em more fac'lty than all the school larnin' in creation. I knowed it was more fillin' than vittles, more rousin' than whiskey, more soothin' than lodlum. I knowed it cooled ye off when ye was het, an' het ye when ye was cold. I knowed all that, o' course — any fool knows it. But —

Fishin' Jimmy

will ye b'l'eve it? — I was more 'n
twenty-one year old, a man growed,
'fore I foun' out why 't was that away.
Father an' mother was Christian folks,
good out-an'-out Calv'nist Baptists
from over East'n way. They fetched
me up right, made me go to meetin'
an' read a chapter every Sunday, an'
say a hymn Sat'day night a'ter washin';
an' I useter say my prayers mos' nights.
I wa'n't a bad boy as boys go. But
nobody thought o' tellin' me the one
thing, jest the one single thing, that 'd
ha' made all the diffunce. I knowed
about God, an' how he made me an'
made the airth, an' everythin', an'
once I got thinkin' about that, an' I
asked my father if God made the
fishes. He said 'course he did, the sea

an' all that in 'em is; but somehow
that did n't seem to mean nothin'
much to me, an' I lost my int'rist agin.
An' I read the Scripter account o'
Jonah an' the big fish, an' all that in
Job about pullin' out levi'thing with
a hook an' stickin' fish-spears in his'
head, an' some parts in them queer
books nigh the end o' the ole Test'-
ment about fish-ponds an' fish-gates an'
fish-pools, an' how the fishers shall
l'ment — everything I could pick out
about fishin' an' sech; but it did n't
come home to me; 't wa'n't my kind
o' fishin' an' I did n't seem ter sense
it.

"But one day — it's more 'n forty
year ago now, but I rec'lect it same 's
't was yest'day, an' I shall rec'lect it

"'T was the ole union meetin'-house."

Fishin' Jimmy

forty thousand year from now if I'm
'round, an' I guess I shall be — I heerd
— suthin' — diffunt. I was down in
the village one Sunday; it wa'n't very
good fishin' — the streams was too full;
an' I thought I'd jest look into the
meetin'-house 's I went by. 'T was
the ole union meetin'-house, down to
the corner, ye know, an' they had n't
got no reg'lar s'pply, an' ye never
knowed what sort ye'd hear, so 't was
kind o' excitin'.

"'T was late, 'most 'leven o'clock,
an' the sarm'n had begun. There was
a strange man a-preachin', some one
from over to the hotel. I never heerd
his name, I never seed him from that
day to this; but I knowed his face.
Queer enough, I'd seed him a-fishin'.

Fishin' Jimmy

I never knowed he was a min'ster; he
did n't look like one.   He went about
like a real fisherman, with ole clo'es
an' an ole hat with hooks stuck in it,
an' big rubber boots, an' he
fished, reely fished, I mean
— ketched 'em. I
guess 't was that
made me
liss'n
a leetle
sharper
'n us'al,
for I

Fishin' Jimmy

never seed a fishin' min'ster afore.
Elder Jacks'n, he said 't was a sinf'l
waste o' time, an' ole Parson Loomis,
he 'd an idee it was cruel an' onmarci-
ful ; so I thought I 'd jest see what
this man 'd preach about, an' I settled
down to liss'n to the sarm'n.

"But there wa'n't no sarm'n ; not
what I 'd been raised to think was the
on'y true kind. There wa'n't no heads,
no fustlys nor sec'ndlys, nor fin'ly
bruthrins, but the first thing I knowed
I was hearin' a story, an' 't was a fishin'
story. 'T was about Some One — I
had n't the least idee then who 't was,
an' how much it all meant — Some
One that was dreffle fond o' fishin' an'
fishermen, Some One that sot everythin' by the water, an' useter go along
by the lakes an' ponds, an' sail on 'em,

27

Fishin' Jimmy

an' talk with the men that was fishin'.
An' how the fishermen all liked him,
'nd asked his 'dvice, an' done jest 's he
telled 'em about the likeliest places to
fish ; an' how they allers ketched more
for mindin' him; an' how when he was
a-preachin' he would n't go into a big
meetin'-house an' talk to rich folks all
slicked up, but he 'd jest go out in a
fishin' boat, an' ask the men to shove
out a mite, an' he 'd talk to the folks on
shore, the fishin' folks an' their wives
an' the boys an' gals playin' on the
shore. An' then, best o' everythin',
he telled how when he was a-choosin'
the men to go about with him an' help
him an' larn his ways so 's to come
a'ter him, he fust o' all picked out the
men he 'd seen every day fishin', an'
mebbe fished with hisself ; for he

knowed 'em an' knowed he could trust 'em.

"An' then he telled us about the day when this preacher come along by the lake — a dreffle sightly place, this min'ster said; he 'd seed it hisself when he was trav'lin' in them countries — an' come acrost two men he knowed well; they was brothers, an' they was a-fishin'. An' he jest asked 'em in his pleasant-spoken, frien'ly way — there wa'n't never sech a drawin', takin', lovin' way with any one afore as this man had, the min'ster said — he jest asked 'em to come along with him; an' they lay down their poles an' their lines an' everythin', an' jined him. An' then he come along a spell further, an' he sees two boys out with their ole father, an' they was settin' in a boat an'

fixin' up their tackle, an' he asked 'em
if they 'd jine him, too, an' they jest
dropped all their things, an' left the ole
man with the boat an' the fish an' the
bait an' follered the preacher. I don't
tell it very good. I 've read it an' read
it sence that ; but I want to make ye
see how it sounded to me, how I took
it, as the min'ster telled it that summer
day in Francony meetin'. Ye see I 'd
no idee who the story was about, the
man put it so plain, in common kind
o' talk, without any come-to-passes an'
whuffers an' thuffers, an' I never con-
ceited 't was a Bible narr'tive.

"An' so fust thing I knowed I says
to myself, 'That 's the kind o' teacher
I want. If I could come acrost a man
like that, I 'd jest foller him, too,
through thick an' thin.' Well, I can't

Fishin' Jimmy

put the rest on it into talk very good;
't aint jest the kind o' thing to speak
on 'fore folks, even sech good friends
as you. I aint the sort to go back on
my word, — fishermen aint, ye know,
— an' what I'd said to myself 'fore I
knowed who I was bindin' myself to,
I stuck to a'terwards when I knowed
all about him. For 't aint for me to
tell ye, who've got so much more
larnin' than me, that there was a dreffle
lot more to that story than the fishin'
part. That lovin', givin' up, suff'rin',
dyin' part, ye know it all yerself, an'
I can't kinder say much on it, 'cept
when I'm jest all by myself, or —
'long o' him.

"That a'ternoon I took my ole
Bible that I had n't read much sence

31

Fishin' Jimmy

I growed up, an' I went out into the
woods 'long the river, an' 'stid o' fishin'
I jest sot down an' read that hull story.
Now ye know it yerself by heart, an'
ye 've knowed it all yer born days, so
ye can't begin to tell how new an'
'stonishin' 't was to me, an' how findin'
so much fishin' in it kinder helped me
unnerstan' an' b'l'eve it every mite, an'
take it right hum to me to foller an'
live up to 's long 's I live an' breathe.
Did j'ever think on it, reely? I tell
ye, his r'liging 's a fishin' r'liging all
through. His friends was fishin' folks;
his pulpit was a fishin' boat, or the
shore o' the lake ; he loved the ponds
an' streams ; an' when his d'sciples
went out fishin', if he did n't go hisself
with 'em, he 'd go a'ter 'em, walkin'

on the water, to cheer 'em up an' comfort 'em.

"An' he was allers 'round the water; for the story 'll say, ' he come to the seashore,' or ' he begun to teach by the seaside,' or agin, ' he entered into a boat,' an' ' he was in the stern o' the boat, asleep.'

"An' he used fish in his mir'cles. He fed that crowd o' folks on fish when they was hungry, bought 'em from a little chap on the shore. I 've oft'n thought how dreffle tickled that boy must 'a' ben to have him take them fish. Mebbe they wa'n't nothin' but shiners, but the fust the little fel- ler 'd ever ketched; an' boys set a heap on their fust ketch. He was dreffle good to child'en, ye know. An' who 'd

he come to a'ter he 'd died, an' ris
agin? Why, he come down to the
shore 'fore daylight, an' looked off
over the pond to where his ole frien's
was a-fishin'. Ye see they 'd gone out
jest to quiet their minds an' keep up
their sperrits; ther 's nothin' like
fishin' for that, ye know, an' they 'd
ben in a heap o' trubble. When they
was settin' up the night afore, worryin'
an' wond'rin' an' s'misin' what was
goin' ter become on 'em without their
master, Peter 'd got kinder desprit, an'
he up an' says in his quick way, says
he, 'Anyway, *I* 'm goin' a-fishin'.'
An' they all see the sense on it, —
any fisherman would, — an' they says,
says they, 'We 'll go 'long too.' But
they did n't ketch anythin'. I sup-

36

Fishin' Jimmy

pose they could n't fix their minds on
it, an' everythin' went wrong like.
But when mornin' come creepin' up
over the mountings, fust thin' they
knowed they see him on the bank,
an' he called out to 'em to know if
they'd ketched anythin'. The water
jest run down my cheeks when I
heerd the min'ster tell that, an' it
kinder makes my eyes wet every time
I think on 't. For 't seems 's if it
might 'a' ben me in that boat, who
heern that v'ice I loved so dreffle
well speak up agin so nat'ral from
the bank there. An' he eat some o'
their fish ! O' course he done it to
sot their minds easy, to show 'em he
wa'n't quite a sperrit yit, but jest their
own ole frien' who'd ben out in the boat
with 'em so many, many times. But

seems to me, jest the fac' he done it
kinder makes fish an' fishin' diffunt
from any other thing in the hull airth.
I tell ye them four books that gin his
story is chock full o' things that go
right to the heart o' fishermen, — nets,
an' hooks, an' boats, an' the shores,
an' the sea, an' the mountings, Peter's
fishin'-coat, lilies, an' sparrers, an' grass
o' the fields, an' all about the evenin'
sky bein' red or lowerin', an' fair or
foul weather.

" It 's an out-doors, woodsy, country
story, 'sides bein' the heav'nliest one
that was ever telled. I read the hull
Bible, as a duty, ye know. I read the
epis'les, but somehow they don't come
home to me. Paul was a great man, a
dreffle smart scholar, but he was raised
in the city, I guess, an' when I go from

Fishin' Jimmy

the gospils into Paul's writin's it's
like goin' from the woods an' hills an'
streams o' Francony into the streets of
a big city like Concord or Manch'ster."

The old man did not say much of
his after life and the fruits of this
strange conversion, but his neighbors
told us a great deal. They spoke of
his unselfishness, his charity, his kindly
deeds ; told of his visiting the poor and
unhappy, nursing the sick. They said
the little children loved him, and every
one in the village and for miles around
trusted and leaned upon Fishin' Jimmy.
He taught the boys to fish, sometimes
the girls too ; and while learning to
cast and strike, to whip the stream,
they drank in knowledge of higher
things, and came to know and love

Fishin' Jimmy

Jimmy's " fishin' r'liging." I remember they told me of a little French Canadian girl, a poor, wretched waif, whose mother, an unknown tramp, had fallen dead in the road near the village. The child, an untamed little heathen, was found clinging to her mother's body in an agony of grief and rage, and fought like a tiger when they tried to take her away. A boy in the little group attracted to the spot ran away, with a child's faith in his old friend, to summon Fishin' Jimmy. He came quickly, lifted the little savage tenderly, and carried her away.

No one witnessed the taming process, but in a few days the pair were seen together on the margin of Black Brook, each with a

Fishin' Jimmy

fish-pole. Her dark face was bright
with interest and excitement as she took
her first lesson in the art of angling.
She jabbered and chattered in her odd
patois, he answered in broadest New
England dialect, but the two quite un-
derstood each other, and though Jimmy
said afterward that it was " dreffle to
hear her call the fish pois'n," they were

soon great friends and comrades. For weeks he kept and cared for the child, and when she left him for a good home in Bethlehem, one would scarcely have recognized in the gentle, affectionate girl the wild creature of the past. Though often questioned as to the means used to effect this change, Jimmy's explanation seemed rather vague and unsatisfactory. "'T was fishin' done it," he said; "on'y fishin'; it allers works. The Christian r'liging itself had to begin with fishin', ye know."

III

BUT one thing troubled Fishin' Jimmy. He wanted to be a " fisher of men." That was what the Great Teacher had promised he would make the fishermen who left their boats to follow him. What strange, literal meaning he attached to the terms, we could not tell. In vain we — especially the boys, whose young hearts had gone out in warm affection to the old man — tried to show him that he was, by his efforts to do good and make others

43

better and happier, fulfilling the Lord's directions. He could not understand it so. "I allers try to think," he said, " that 't was me in that boat when he come along. I make b'l'eve that it was out on Streeter Pond, an' I was settin' in the boat, fixin' my lan'in' net, when I see him on the shore. I think mebbe I'm that James — for that's my given name, ye know, though they allers call me Jimmy — an' then I hear him callin' me, 'James, James.' I can hear him jest's plain sometimes, when the wind's blowin' in the trees, an' I jest ache to up an' foller him. But says he, 'I'll make ye a fisher o' men,' an' he aint done it. I'm waitin'; mebbe he'll larn me some day."

He was fond of all living creatures,

" *An'* I was settin' in the boat, fixin' my lan'in' net,
when I see him on the shore."

Fishin' Jimmy

merciful to all. But his love for our dog Dash became a passion, for Dash was an angler. Who that ever saw him sitting in the boat beside his master, watching with eager eye and whole body trembling with excitement the line as it was cast, the flies as they touched the surface — who can forget old Dash? His fierce excitement at rise of trout, the efforts at self-restraint, the disappointment if the prey escaped, the wild exultation if it was captured,

47

how plainly — he who runs might read
— were shown these emotions in eye, in
ear, in tail, in whole quivering body!
What wonder that it all went straight
to the fisher's heart of Jimmy! "I
never knowed afore they could be
Christians," he said, looking, with tears
in his soft, keen eyes, at the every-day
scene, and with no faintest thought of
irreverence. "I never knowed it, but
I'd give a stiffikit o' membership in
the orthodoxest church goin' to that
dog there."

It is almost needless to say that as
years went on Jimmy came to know
many "fishin' min'sters;" for there
are many of that school who know our
mountain country, and seek it yearly.
All these knew and loved the old man.

Fishin' Jimmy

And there were others who had wandered by that Sea of Galilee, and fished in the waters of the Holy Land, and with them Fishin' Jimmy dearly loved to talk. But his wonder was never-ending that, in the scheme of evangelizing the world, more use was not made of the "fishin' side" of the story. " Haint they ever tried it on them poor heathen?" he would ask earnestly of some clerical angler casting a fly upon the clear water of pond or brook. " I should think 't would 'a' ben the fust thing they 'd done. Fishin' fust, an' r'liging 's sure to foller. An' it 's so easy; fur heath'n mostly r'sides on islands, don't they? So ther 's plenty o' water, an' o' course ther 's fishin'; an' oncet gin 'em poles an' git 'em to

work, an' they 're out o' mischief fur
that day. They 'd like it better 'n
cannib'ling, or cuttin' out idles, or
scratchin' picters all over theirselves,
an' bimeby — not too suddent, ye
know, to scare 'em — ye could begin
on that story, an' they could n't stan'
that, not a heath'n on 'em. Won't ye
speak to the 'Merican Board about it,
an' sen' out a few fishin' mishneries, with
poles an' lines an' tackle gen'ally? I 've
tried it on dreffle bad folks, an' it allers
done 'em good. But " — so almost all
his simple talk ended — " I wish I
could begin to be a fisher o' men. I 'm
gettin' on now, I 'm nigh seventy, an'
I aint got much time, ye see."

One afternoon in July there came
over Franconia Notch one of those

Fishin' Jimmy

strangely sudden tempests which sometimes visit that mountain country. It
had been warm that day, unusually
warm for that refreshingly cool spot;
but suddenly the sky grew dark and
darker, almost to blackness, there was
roll of thunder and flash of lightning,
and then poured down the rain — rain
at first, but soon hail in large frozen
bullets, which fiercely pelted any who
ventured outdoors, rattled against the
windows of the Profile House with
sharp cracks like sounds of musketry,
and lay upon the piazza in heaps like
snow. And in the midst of the wild
storm it was remembered that two
boys, guests at the hotel, had gone
up Mount Lafayette alone that day.
They were young boys, unused to

mountain climbing, and their friends
were anxious. It was found that Dash
had followed them; and just as some
one was to be sent in search of them, a
boy from the stables brought the infor-
mation that Fishin' Jimmy had started
up the mountain after them as the
storm broke. " Said if he could n't be a
fisher o' men, mebbe he knowed nuff to
ketch boys," went on our informant,
seeing nothing more in the speech, full
of pathetic meaning to us who knew
him, than the idle talk of one whom
many considered " lackin'." Jimmy
was old now, and had of late grown
very feeble, and we did not like to
think of him out in that wild storm.
And now suddenly the lost boys themselves appeared through the opening in

Fishin' Jimmy

the woods opposite the house, and ran
in through the sleet, now falling more
quietly.   They were wet, but no worse
apparently for their adventure, though
full of contrition and distress at having
lost sight of the dog.   He had rushed
off into the woods some hours before,
after a rabbit or hedgehog, and had
never returned.   Nor had they seen
Fishin' Jimmy.

As hours went by and the old man
did not return, a search party was
sent out, and guides familiar with the
mountain paths went up Lafayette to
seek for him.   It was nearly night
when they at last found him, and the
grand old mountains had put on those
robes of royal purple which they sometimes assume at eventide.   At the foot

of a mass of rock, which looked like
amethyst or wine-red agate in that
marvellous evening light, the old man
was lying, and Dash was with him.
From the few faint words Jimmy could
then gasp out, the truth was gathered.
He had missed the boys, leaving the
path by which they had returned, and
while stumbling along in search of
them, feeble and weary, he had heard
far below a sound of distress. Looking down over a steep, rocky ledge, he
had seen his friend and fishing com-
rade, old Dash, in sore trouble. Poor
Dash ! He never dreamed of harming
his old friend, for he had a kind heart.
But he was a sad coward in some mat-
ters, and a very baby when frightened
and away from master and friends. So

" It was nearly night when they at last found him."

Fishin' Jimmy

I fear he may have assumed the rôle of wounded sufferer when in reality he was but scared and lonesome. He never owned this afterward, and you may be sure we never let him know, by word or look, the evil he had done. Jimmy saw him holding up one paw helplessly, and looking at him with wistful, imploring brown eyes, heard his pitiful whimpering cry for aid, and never doubted his great distress and peril. Was Dash not a fisherman? And fishermen, in Fishin' Jimmy's category, were always true and trusty. So the old man without a second's hesitation started down the steep, smooth decline to the rescue of his friend.

We do not know just how or where in that terrible descent he fell. To

Fishin' Jimmy

us who afterward saw the spot, and
thought of the weak old man, chilled
by the storm, exhausted by his exer-
tions, and yet clambering down that
precipitous cliff, made more slippery
and treacherous by the sleet and hail
still falling, it seemed impossible that
he could have kept a foothold for an
instant. Nor am I sure that he ex-
pected to save himself, and Dash too.
But he tried. He was sadly hurt. I
will not tell you of that.

Looking out from the hotel windows
through the gathering darkness, we who
loved him — it was not a small group
— saw a sorrowful sight. Flickering
lights thrown by the lanterns of
the guides came through the woods.
Across the road, slowly, carefully,

came strong men, bearing on a rough,
hastily made litter of boughs the dear
old man. All that could have been
done for the most distinguished guest,
for the dearest, best-beloved friend, was
done for the gentle fisherman. We,
his friends, and proud to style our-
selves thus, were of different, widely
separated lands, greatly varying creeds.
Some were nearly as old as the dying
man, some in the prime of manhood.
There were youths and maidens and
little children. But through the night
we watched together. The old Roman
bishop, whose calm, benign face we
all know and love; the Churchman,
ascetic in faith, but with the kindest,
most indulgent heart when one finds
it; the gentle old Quakeress with

Fishin' Jimmy

placid, unwrinkled brow and silvery
hair; Presbyterian, Methodist, and
Baptist, — we were all one that night.
The old angler did not suffer — we
were so glad of that! But he did not
appear to know us, and his talk seemed
strange. It rambled on quietly, softly,
like one of his own mountain brooks,
babbling of green fields, of sunny summer days, of his favorite sport, and ah!
of other things. But he was not speak-
ing to us. A sudden, awed hush and
thrill came over us as, bending to catch
the low words, we all at once under-
stood what only the bishop put into
words as he said, half to himself, in a
sudden, quick, broken whisper, "God
bless the man, he's talking to his
Master!"

Fishin' Jimmy

"Yes, sir, that 's so," went on the
quiet voice; "'t was on'y a dog sure
nuff; 't wa'n't even a boy, as ye say,
an' ye ast me to be a fisher o' men.
But I haint had no chance for that,
somehow ; mebbe I wa'n't fit
for 't. I 'm on'y jest a poor
old fisherman, Fishin' Jimmy,
ye know, sir. Ye useter call
me James — no one else
ever done it. On'y a dog ?
But he wa'n't jest a common
dog, sir ; he was a fishin' dog. I
never seed a man love fishin' mor'n
Dash." The dog was in the room,
and heard his name. Stealing to
the bedside, he put a cold nose into
the cold hand of his old friend, and
no one had the heart to take him away.

Fishin' Jimmy

The touch turned the current of the old man's talk for a moment, and he was fishing again with his dog friend. "See 'em break, Dashy! See 'em break! Lots on 'em to-day, aint they? Keep still, there's a good dog, while I put on a diffunt fly. Don't ye see they're jumpin' at them gnats? Aint the water jest 'live with 'em? Aint it shinin' an' clear an' —" The voice faltered an instant, then went on: "Yes, sir, I'm comin' — I'm glad, dreffle glad to come. Don't mind 'bout my leavin' my fishin'; do ye think I care 'bout that? I 'll jest lay down my pole ahin' the alders here, an' put my lan'in' net on the stuns, with my flies an' tackle — the boys 'll like 'em, ye know — an' I 'll be right along.

" He put a cold nose into the cold hand of his old friend."

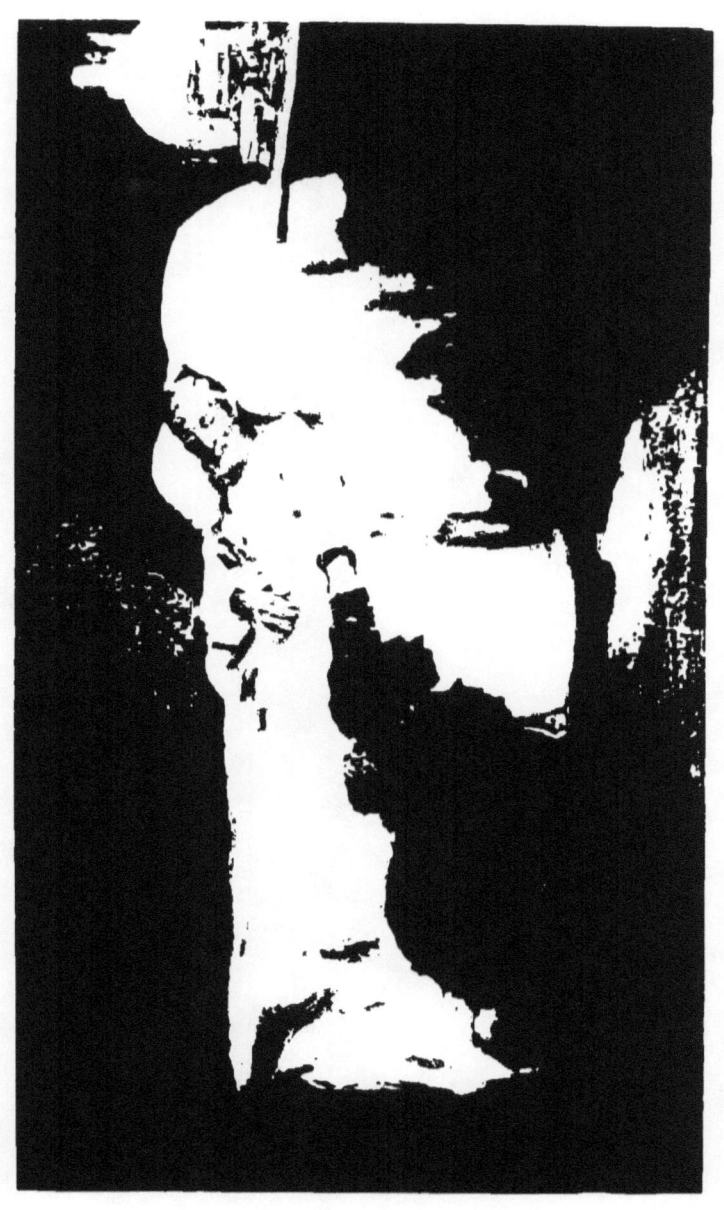

Fishin' Jimmy

"I mos' knowed ye was on'y a-tryin'
me when ye said that 'bout how I
had n't been a fisher o' men, nor even
boys, on'y a dog. 'T was a — fishin'
dog — ye know — an' ye was allers
dreffle good to fishermen, — dreffle
good to — everybody ; died — for 'em,
did n't ye ? —

" Please wait — on — the bank there,
a minnit ; I 'm comin' 'crost. Water
's pretty — cold this — spring — an'
the stream 's risin' — but — I — can —
do it ; — don't ye mind — 'bout me,
sir. I 'll get acrost." Once more the
voice ceased, and we thought we should
not hear it again this side that stream.

But suddenly a strange light came
over the thin face, the soft gray eyes
opened wide, and he cried out, with the

5   65

Fishin' Jimmy

strong voice we had so often heard
come ringing out to us across the
mountain streams above the sound of
their rushing : " Here I be, sir ! It 's
Fishin' Jimmy, ye know, from Francony way ; him ye useter call James
when ye come 'long the shore o' the
pond an' I was a-fishin'. I heern ye
agin, jest now — an' I — straight-
way — f'sook — my — nets — an' —
follered — "

Had the voice ceased utterly ? No,
we could catch faint, low murmurs and
the lips still moved. But the words
were not for us ; and we did not know
when he reached the other bank.

66